Sports Illustrated KIDS

GOODNIGHT FOOTBALL

BY MICHAEL DAHL   ILLUSTRATED BY CHRISTINA FORSHAY

PICTURE WINDOW BOOKS
A CAPSTONE IMPRINT

It's the end of the week,
it's the best of all sights —
beneath the night sky
lies a field of bright lights!

And the bleachers are full, for a very good reason.

The big game is tonight! It's football season!

The big band plays, and the cheerleaders shout!

And everyone cheers as the teams run out!

The fans are excited.
It's time for some fun!

On third and one, the ball is snapped.

But the defense breaks through, and the quarterback's sacked!

He shakes it off and gets up,
the crowd yells, "Hooray!"

Then the team
huddles up
and discusses
a play.

The quarterback drops back and lets the ball go.

It sails through the air.

Oh, what a throw!

A receiver breaks loose and stands all alone . . .

reaches up . . .
grabs the ball . . .

he's in the end zone!

The teams trade possessions,
up and down rolls the score.

Then a long run wins the game —
hear the crowd ROAR!

What a game! What a night!

Goodnight, players. You fought a good fight.

Goodnight coaches, as they shake hands.

Goodnight, cheerleaders.

Goodnight, band.

Goodnight, bleachers.

Goodnight, fans.

Goodnight field and concession stands.

Goodnight, mascot.

We'll come back soon.

Goodnight, goalposts.
Goodnight, moon.

Goodnight helmet
and my favorite
teams . . .

Goodnight, football.
Goodnight and sweet dreams.

TO DANNY THOMAS.

Published by
PICTURE WINDOW BOOKS
a Capstone imprint
1710 Roe Crest Drive, North Mankato, Minnesota 56003

www.capstonepub.com

Library of Congress Cataloging-in-Publication data is
available on the Library of Congress website.

ISBN: 978-1-62370-106-2 (hardcover)
ISBN: 978-1-4795-5177-4 (library binding)
ISBN: 978-1-4795-5186-6 (paperback)
ISBN: 978-1-4795-55962-6 (ebook)

Designer: Bob Lentz

Printed and bound in the USA.
3455